Bitsy, the Bu

~Minnesota~

by Linda Francis and Judy Kvaale

Illustrated by
McCal Joy

This book is dedicated to
our teaching colleagues who have
given us support throughout this venture.

***Note**: Look for a hidden fall leaf on each page.*
(Colors will vary.)

Other books in the Gingerbread Cousins series:

Miki, the Mixed Up Musher ~ Alaska ~
Skip, the Spacey Surfer ~ Florida ~
Cash, the Carefree Cowboy ~ North Dakota ~
Tanner, the Timely Traveler ~ Pennsylvania ~
Diego, the Distance Driver ~ Arizona ~

ISBN-10: 978-1515153153
ISBN-13: 1515153150

September 20
Dear Gingerbread Man,
Hi Cuz! I just read the book about your exciting adventures. Oh, for fun! It reminds me of what happened last week. Let me tell you about it...

It was a beautiful day in Little Falls. The town was full of vendors for the Arts and Crafts Fair.

Victor, the vocal vender, was busy setting up his "Sweet Treats" food stand. As he was unpacking his frosted gingerbread cookies, I stunned him by hopping out of his hand.

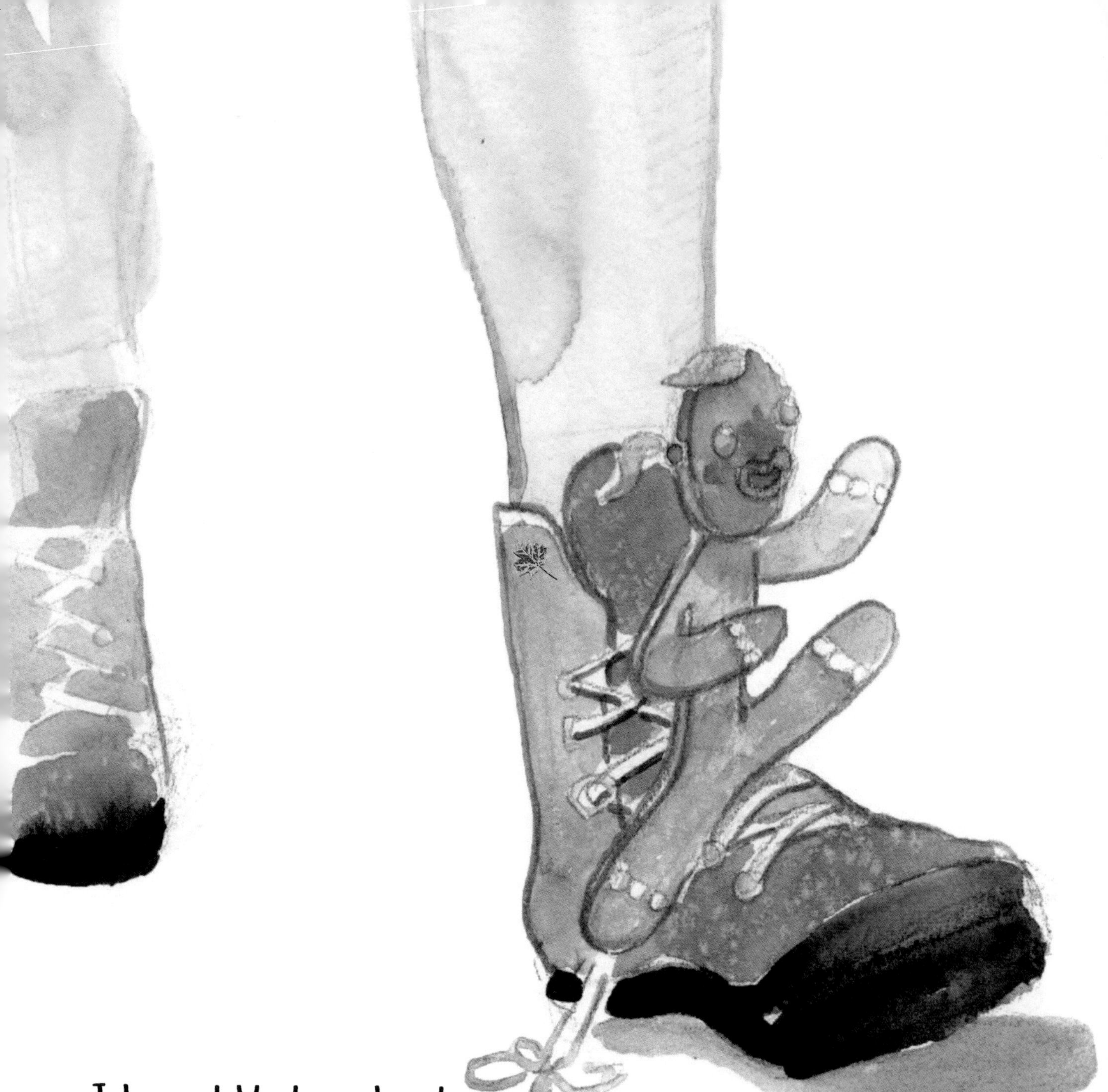

I heard Victor shout
in his loud voice, "Come back, little gingerbread girl!"

I skedaddled down the street,
and what should I see...

But a bike and helmet
waiting for me.

I couldn't believe my eyes! I put on my helmet, hopped on the bike, and chanted:

"Pedal, pedal and give it a whirl!
You can't catch me.
I'm a Gingerbread Girl!"

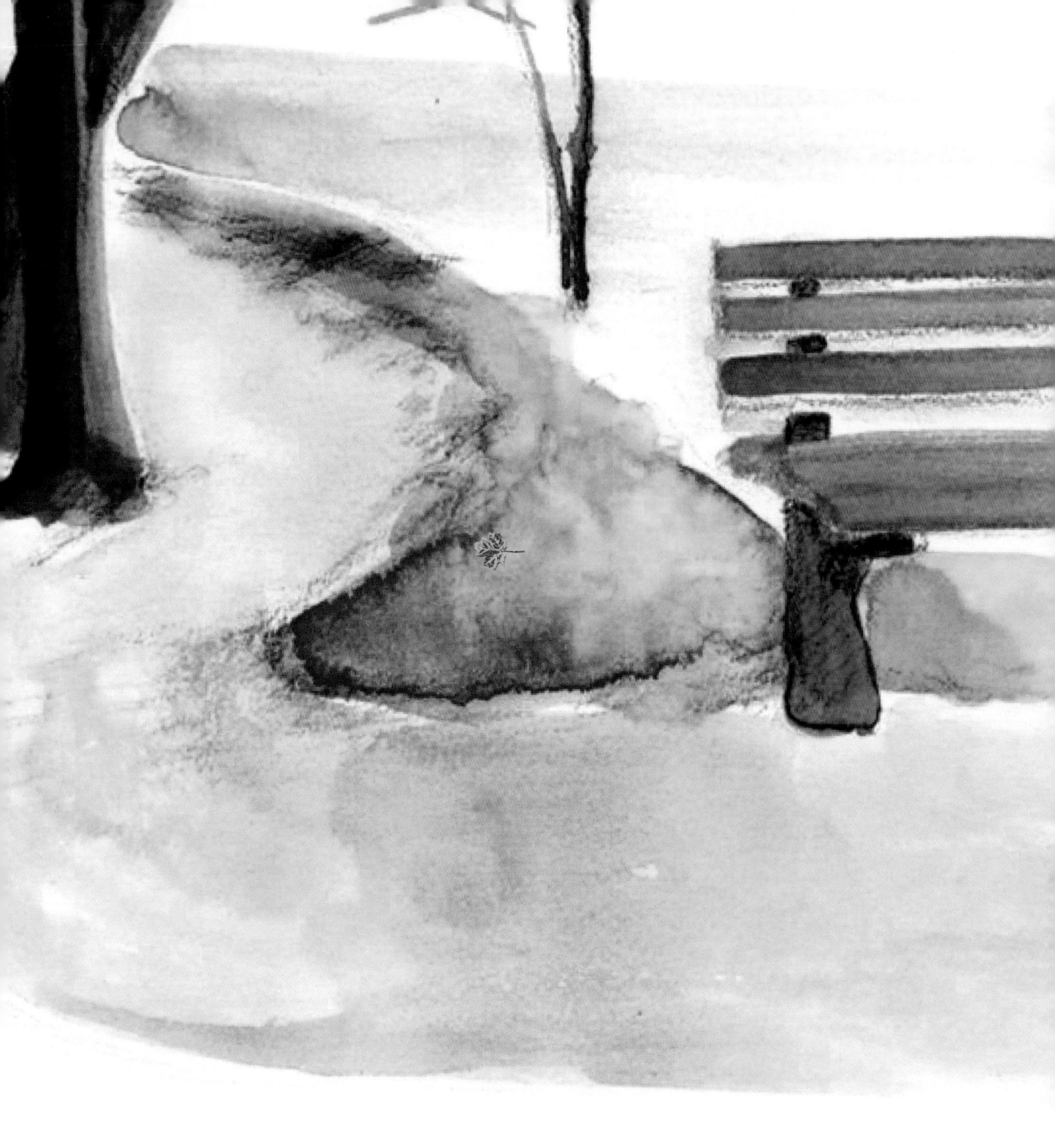

I pedaled and I pedaled on the Mississippi River Bike Trail. I stopped to take a break by the river, and what should I see...

But an **odd otter**
observing me.

I saw the intense look in its eyes
and knew I had to pedal on.

So I chanted:

"Observe, observe and give it a whirl!
You can't catch me.
I'm a Gingerbread Girl!

I can pedal away from **vocal Victor**,
And I can pedal away from you, I can!"

I jumped on my bike and continued on the trail to Hackensack. There I saw a statue of Lucette. I sat down, and suddenly I heard a splashing sound.

I turned around, and what should I see...

But a **whopping walleye**
weaving toward me.

I saw the mean look in its eyes
and knew I had to pedal on.

So I chanted:

"Weave, weave and give it a whirl!
You can't catch me.
I'm a Gingerbread Girl!

I can pedal away from **vocal Victor**,
and an **odd otter**; and I can pedal away
from you, I can!"

I pedaled and I pedaled through
the quiet countryside,

until what should I see...

But powerful Paul Bunyan beckoning me.

I saw the hungry look in his eyes
and knew I had to pedal on.

So I chanted:

"Beckon, beckon and give it a whirl!
You can't catch me.
I'm a Gingerbread Girl!

I can pedal away from **vocal Victor**,
an **odd otter** and a **whopping walleye**;
And I can pedal away from you, I can!"

I pedaled and I pedaled into Itasca Park
when suddenly I heard a mournful sound,

and then what should I see...

But a lonely loon
looking at me.

I saw the cautious look in its eyes
and knew I had to pedal on.

So I chanted:

"Look, look and give it a whirl!
You can't catch me.
I'm a Gingerbread Girl!

I can pedal away from **vocal Victor**, an **odd otter**, a **whopping walleye** and **powerful Paul Bunyan**; and I can pedal away from you, I can!"

I pedaled and I pedaled until
I reached the Headwaters of
the Mississippi River.

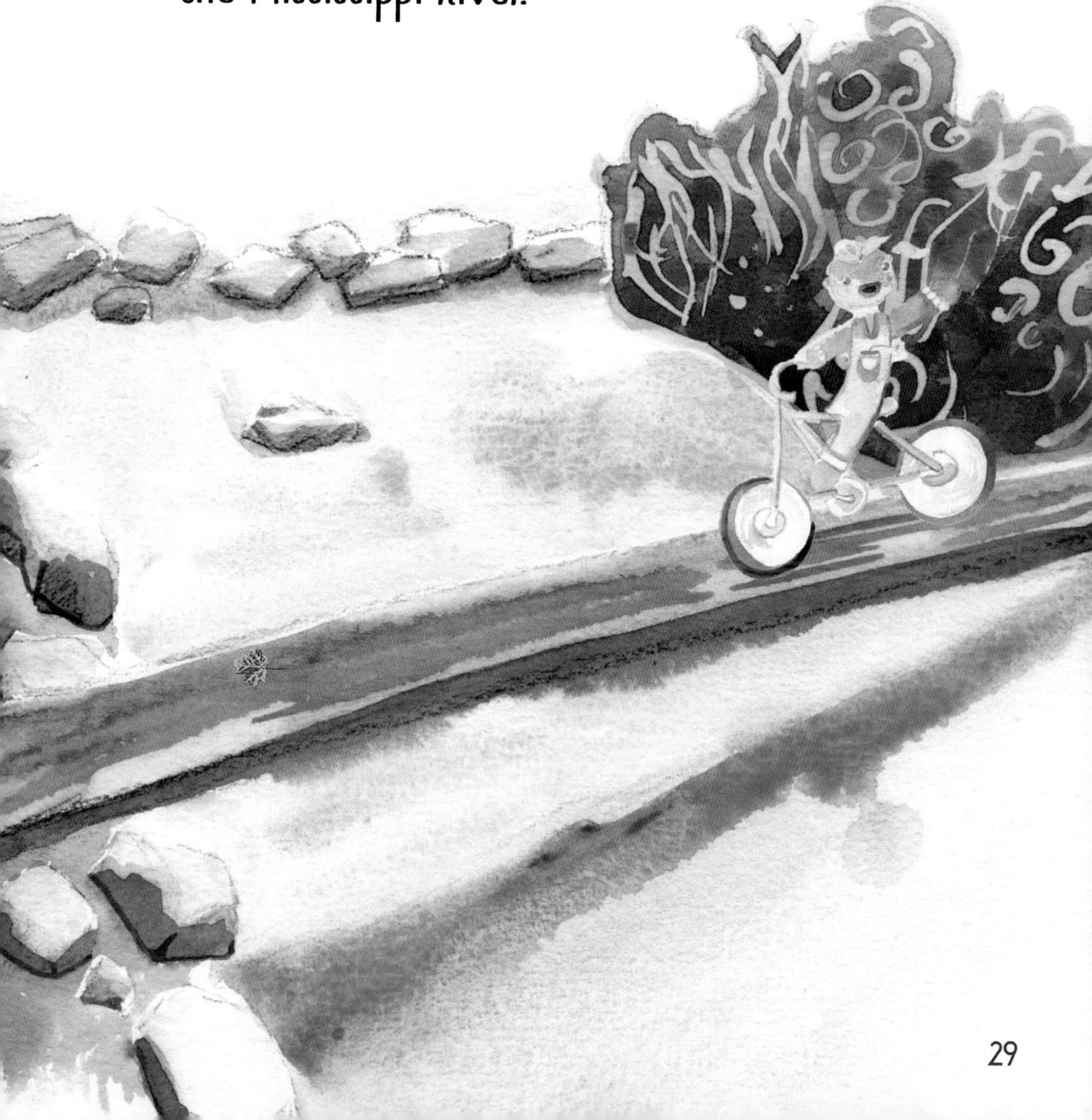

I jumped off my bike and tiptoed
across the slippery rocks,

and then what should I see...

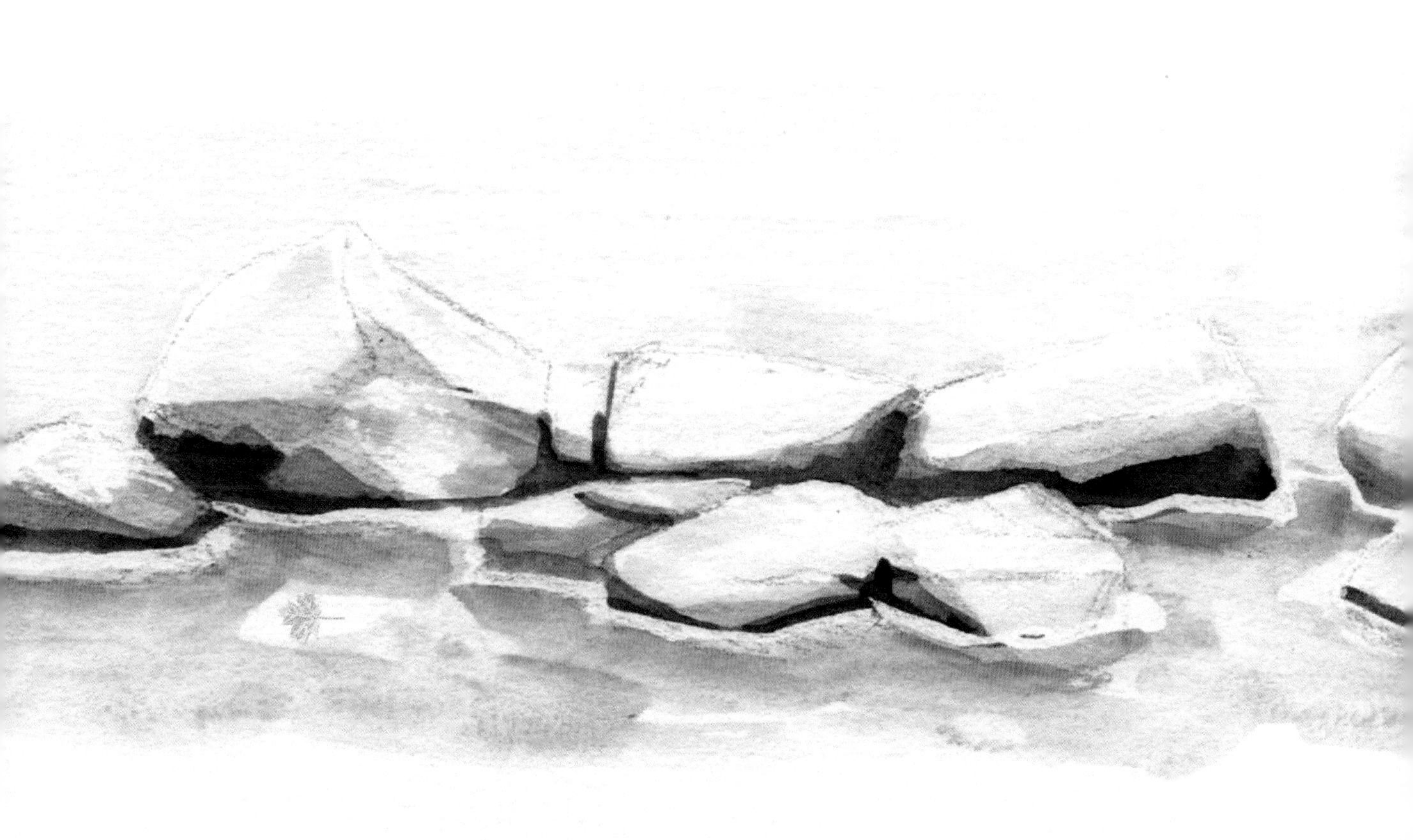

But a **proud Park Ranger** running toward me. I saw the excited look in his eyes.

When he gave me
a ranger hat,

I then realized,

I was going to be his assistant for the day!

What an awesome adventure! I think I would like to be a park ranger. I wonder what other responsibilities I'd be assigned. Have you heard from any of our other cousins?

Gotta go,

Your cousin from Minnesota,
Bitsy, the Busy Biker

Minnesota Facts

The fiberglass Paul Bunyan statue in Akeley, MN is 30 1/2 feet tall. Paul bends down on one knee so people can sit in his hand. Paul Bunyan, a folk lore legend, was a giant lumberjack who traveled the north woods with Babe the Blue Ox.

The small carved wooden statue of Paul Bunyan in Hackensack stands near the bike trail named for him.

The fiberglass statue of Lucette Diana Kensack in Hackensack is 17 feet tall. Legend states that Lucette is the sweetheart of Paul Bunyan. When it gets cold in the winter, the residents will wrap a scarf around her neck!

Itasca Park, the oldest park in Minnesota, has 100 lakes. You can walk across the source of the Mississippi River here.

PHOTOGRAPH courtesy of Jill Wehlander

About the Authors

Judy Kvaale and **Linda Francis** are retired teachers who recognize the importance of instilling the love of reading in children. Linda was a kindergarten teacher for 34 years, and Judy was a third grade teacher for 29 years. Both Linda and Judy live in West Fargo, North Dakota.

The idea of writing a children's book originated during one of their morning walks.

For more information on our books:
gcbooks.weebly.com
or GC Books on Facebook

The Illustrator

McCal Joy is a Fargo artist that is often found in her studio perched over Broadway, Downtown Fargo. She creates as a way to reiterate tales and stories. Her artwork is inspired by history, folklore, whimsical tales, and events that are impactful. She believes that everyone should take the time to stop and create something meaningful once in a while.

website: www.mccaljoy.com

Made in the USA
Charleston, SC
08 June 2016